GREENWILLOW BOOKS
AN IMPRINT OF
HARPERCOLLINSPUBLISHERS

Fox and the Box

STORY AND PICTURES BY

YVONNE IVINSON

Fox and the Box
Copyright © 2019 by Yvonne Ivinson
All rights reserved. Manufactured in China. For information address
HarperCollins Children's Books, a division of HarperCollins Publishers,
195 Broadway, New York, NY 10007.
www.harpercollinschildrens.com

Acrylic paint was used to prepare the full-color art. The text type is Century Gothic.

Library of Congress Cataloging-in-Publication Data

Names: Ivinson, Yvonne, author, illustrator.
Title: Fox and the box / by Yvonne Ivinson.
Description: First edition. | New York, NY : Greenwillow Books, an imprint of HarperCollins Publishers, 2019. |
Summary: A fox sets out across the sea in a floating box on a grand adventure full of endless possibilities.
Identifiers: LCCN 2018041414 | ISBN 9780062842879 (hardcover)
Subjects: | CYAC: Stories in rhyme. | Foxes—Fiction. | Seafaring life—Fiction. | Adventure and
    adventurers—Fiction. | BISAC: JUVENILE FICTION / Animals / Foxes. | JUVENILE FICTION / Imagination & Play. |
    JUVENILE FICTION / Readers / Beginner.
Classification: LCC PZ8.3.I835 Fo 2019 | DDC [E]—dc23 LC record available
    at https://lccn.loc.gov/2018041414
19 20 21 22 23 SCP 10 9 8 7 6 5 4 3 2 1
First Edition

Greenwillow Books

For Mum, who bought all my paints
and brushes when I was growing up,
and for Adrian, without whom
there would be no *Fox*

Fox.

Box.

Sail.

Tail.

Oh no!
Tail
sail
fail.

Sail for sale.

Shell.
Sell?

Nail sail.

Ship. Trip.

Don't tip!

Boat.

Float.

Fox.
Box.
Sail.

Oh no!
Hail!
Gale!

Tossed.

Lost?

Pail.
Bail.

See. Sea.

Help me!

Spout. Shout!

Turn about.

Thank you,

big blue whale.